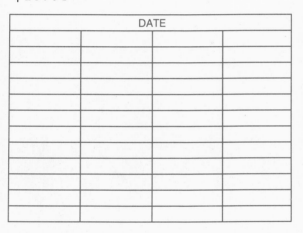

JUV/E
FIC

McPhail, David M.

Yesterday I lost a
sneaker (and found
the Great Goob
sick)

$13.95

DATE			

Yesterday I Lost a Sneaker

(and Found the Great Goob Sick)

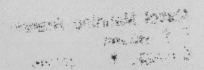

© 1995 Silver Burdett Press
© Copyright, 1985, 1973, by Ginn and Company
Theodore Clymer, adviser

Published by Silver Press,
an imprint of Silver Burdett Press,
A Simon & Schuster Company
299 Jefferson Road, Parsippany, NJ 07054

Printed in the United States of America

10 9 8 7 6 5 4 3 2 1

Library of Congress Cataloging-in-Publication Data

McPhail, David M.
Yesterday I lost a sneaker (and found the Great Goob
sick)/by David McPhail; illustrated by David McPhail.
p. cm.
Summary: A boy goes into his neighbor's yard to help
the very sick, very hungry Great Goob and ends up
with a missing sneaker and a stomachache.
[1. Monsters—Fiction.   2. Imagination—Fiction.
3. Food habits—Fiction.]   I. Title.
PZ7.M4788184Ye 1995
[E]--dc20   94-22862   CIP   AC
ISBN 0-382-24905-4 (LSB)   ISBN 0-382-24906-2 (JHC)
ISBN 0-382-24907-0 (S/C)

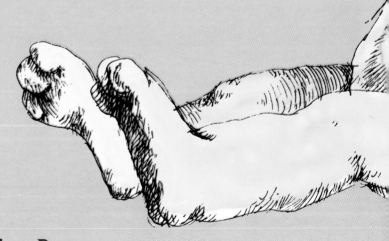

Silver Press

Parsippany, New Jersey

Yesterday I Lost a Sneaker

(and Found the Great Goob Sick)

written and illustrated by David McPhail

Yesterday I lost a sneaker . . .
and I couldn't wait to get home and tell
my mother.

"Mom," I said. "You'll never guess what happened."

"What happened to your other sneaker?" she asked.

"That's what you'll never guess," I said.

"To save time," she said, "why don't you just tell me."

So I did.

I was playing in the backyard near
the fence when I heard a noise in Mr.
Crabtree's yard.

I would have climbed over the fence
to find out what was making the noise . . .
but I knew I shouldn't go into Mr.
Crabtree's yard.

Then I heard the noise again. Only this time it was louder.

"Someone must be sick," I said to myself. "I'd better go and see."

So I climbed over the fence into Mr. Crabtree's yard.

I looked around, but no one was there.
I looked in the pine trees, but no one
was there either.

Then I looked behind the hedge . . .
and someone was there!
"Hello," I said. "Who are you?"

"Ooooowwwww," he said. "I'm the Great Goob, and I'm so sick."

"I'll get help," I said.

"Nooooooo," he said. "What I need is some carrots from Mr. Crabtree's garden."

"But I can't take carrots from Mr. Crabtree's garden," I said.

"Ooooowwwww," said the Great Goob.
So I went into Mr. Crabtree's garden
and took some carrots.

When the Great Goob had eaten the carrots, I asked him if he was feeling any better.

"Nooooooo," he said. "Perhaps some of Mr. Crabtree's peaches will help."

"Oh," I said. "But I can't take any of Mr. Crabtree's peaches."

"Ooooooooowwwwwwww," he said.

So I climbed Mr. Crabtree's peach tree and picked some peaches. When the Great Goob had finished the peaches, I asked him if he was feeling any better.

"Nooooooo," he said. "But maybe some of Mr. Crabtree's grapes will help."

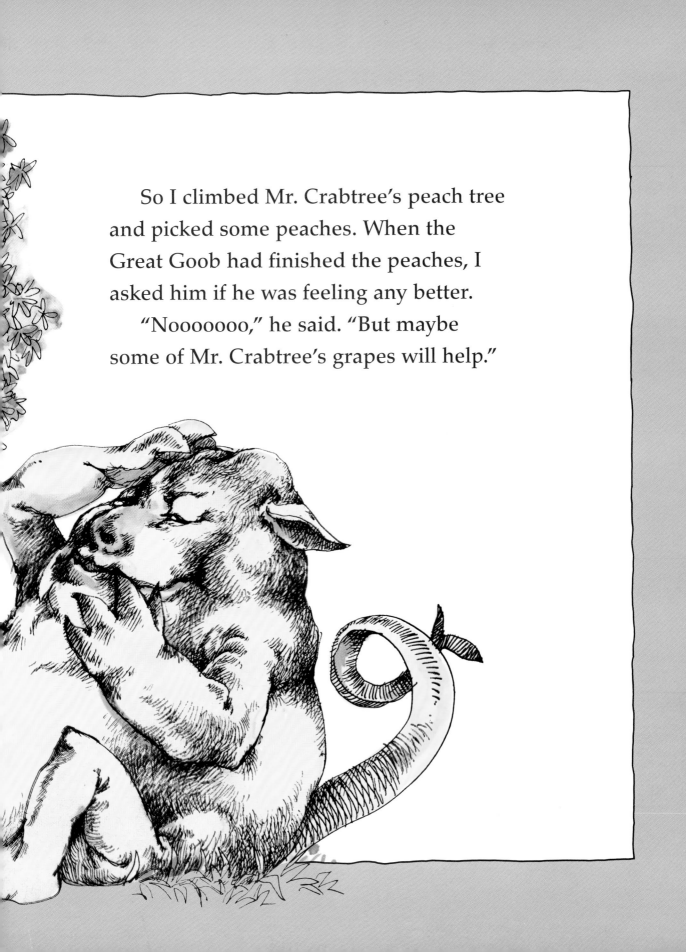

"Oh," I said. "I can't take any of Mr. Crabtree's grapes."

"Oooooooowwwwww," said the Great Goob.

So I picked some of Mr. Crabtree's grapes and gave them to him.

While the Great Goob was eating the grapes, I heard Mr. Crabtree's dog barking.

"If that dog finds us, he'll eat us up," I said. "Let's go over to my yard."

But the Great Goob was too sick to walk . . . so I had to carry him.

When we got to the fence, I boosted the Great Goob over.

And just as I was climbing over . . .

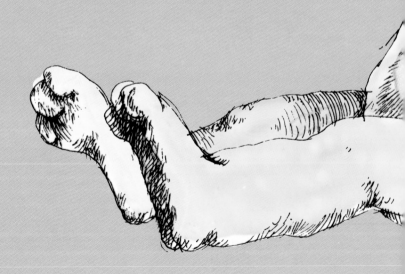

Mr. Crabtree's dog came and bit my
sneaker . . . and yanked it off!

"But I saved the Great Goob," I said. "And he was feeling so much better that he went home.

"That's how I lost my sneaker, Mom. Now can I go to my room?"

"I don't feel so good."

David McPhail wanted to be an artist from the time he was very young. Sometimes his wish led to trouble, however. "Drawing on walls was not acceptable," he remembers, "nor was drawing during school, except in art class."

When he wasn't drawing, he played sports or spent his days at the beach and in the woods near his home in Newburyport, Massachusetts.

Mr. McPhail published his first book, *The Bear's Toothache*, in 1972. Since then he has written and illustrated more than forty books, including several award winners.

Mr. McPhail lives in the house where he grew up. He still enjoys sports, the woods and beach and, of course, drawing.